CIRRUS CLOUDS

FUJITA scale
RATES TORNADO INTENSITY

F0	40-72 mph	**GALE**
F1	73-112 mph	**MODERATE**
F2	113-157 mph	**CONSIDERABLE**
F3	158-206 mph	**EXTREME**
F4	207-260 mph	**DEVASTATING**
F5	261-318 mph	**INCREDIBLE**
	319-375 mph	**INCONCEIVABLE**

B. Taurus: **BESSIE**

H. Sapiens: **BAILEY**

TORNADO ALLEY

INCLUDES TX OK ...TWISTERS OCCUR throughout NORTH AMERICA and the world

dearest Oman
You are three!
Oh my!
Happy happy!
and best wishes!
Love always—
Sash and Dagie

For Ma and Pa,

With a tip o' the hat to the Bozeman Writers Group.

C. F.

THIS IS A BORZOI BOOK PUBLISHED BY ALFRED A. KNOPF

Published in the United States of America by Alfred A. Knopf,

a division of Random House, Inc., New York,

and simultaneously in Canada by Random House of Canada Limited, Toronto.

Distributed by Random House, Inc., New York.

KNOPF, BORZOI BOOKS, and the colophon are registered trademarks of Random House, Inc.

www.randomhouse.com/kids   www.carolynfisher.com

Library of Congress Cataloging-in-Publication Data

Fisher, Carolyn, 1968–

A Twisted Tale / by Carolyn Fisher

p.   cm.

Summary: After a tornado hits Bailey Tarbell's family farm,
all the animals are mixed up and it takes some creative thinking
for Bailey to get things straightened out - almost!

ISBN 0-375-81540-6 (trade) – ISBN 0-375-91540-0 (lib. bdg.)

[1. Domestic animals - Fiction. 2. Tornadoes - Fiction.

3. Humorous stories.]

I. Title.

Pz7.F4994 Tw 2002

[E]- dc 21

Printed in the United States of America

May 2002

10 9 8 7 6 5 4 3 2 1

A Twisted Tale

BY CAROLYN FISHER

Alfred A. Knopf • New York

BAILEY TARBELL lived on a FARM

with

her ma,

her pa...

One day, a sudden gust of wind blew up from the west. Bailey glanced at the sky. "Yippety-yodle-eye-hay, there's a twister coming!" she cried.

Quick as spit, Bailey herded the animals into the barn. Then she ran down to the storm cellar with Ma and Pa.

The wind howled like a prom queen steppin' on a cow patty.

It tore the roof right off the barn and whirled those animals into the air.

The cow's eyes bulged.

The cat's fur

The pig's knuckles turned white.

Stood on end.

Then that twister spat out the critters like a cowpoke spits out a wad of chew.

When the wind blew away,

Bailey burst out of the storm cellar just in time

to see the cow fly over to the chicken coop

and sit on the nests. "Cluck, cluck!" she squawked.

"Quack, quack!" rasped the pig.

She dove into the pond.

The duck chewed its cud.

The chickens wallowed in the mud.

The cat chased the dog, who climbed up a tree and yowled. "Well, I'll be hornswoggled!" cried Bailey.

"The twister mixed up the animals."

ccclucKacluckKacluck

"Jumpin' Jehoshaphat!" Pa said.
"What are we going to do?"
Bailey said, "Let's call the vet."

So Ma phoned Doc Smoot, who looked at
the animals and scratched his chin.
"It's plumb peculiar!" Doc Smoot said.
He took their temperatures.
He peered into their ears.
He fed them large red pills.
But nothing changed. Doc
Smoot shrugged and went away.

Bailey did everything she could to cure the animals.
She demonstrated animal behavior.
(Ma and Pa helped.)

Bailey even tried hypnosis.
Nothing Worked.

Bailey was baffled. Meanwhile, the cow perched on the roof and Crowed.

The chickens **rooted** in the
MUD.

The cat gnawed a bone,
the dog chased mice,
and the pig
was as wrinkled
as a raisin.

Then one day, as Bailey got out of her bath, she twirled a towel around her head and watched the water SWIRL down the drain.

"Eureka!" she cried. "That's it."

She told Ma and Pa her plan. They loaded the animals into the truck and drove to the nearest...

They flew on the Ferris Wheel.

They crashed through the Cannonball.

But they were still mixed up.

Then Bailey saw a ride
that was **bigger** than the rest.
"Why, I'll be hopped!"
Bailey said. "It's the **Twister!**"

"Yodle-yippety-hay-eye!"

shouted Bailey.

When the Twister
jolted to a stop,

Bailey and the animals

stumbled back to the truck.

As Pa drove home, they listened to the right sounds coming from the cow, the cat, the dog, the duck, three chickens, and a pig.

meeooooowW

QUACKQUACK

Oooink

oinkoink

cluckcluck

cluckcluckcluck

CLUCKCLUCKCLUCKCLUCKCLUCK

MOOOOOO